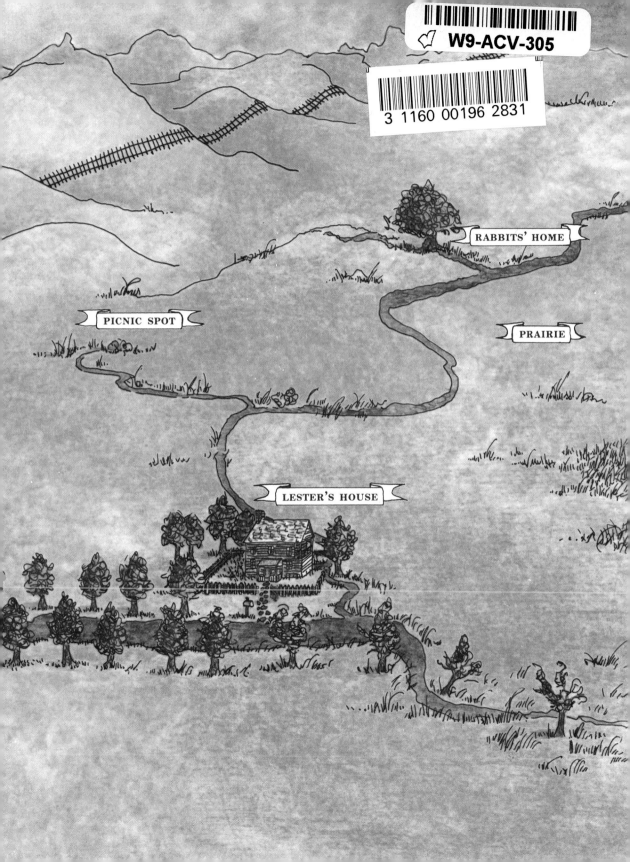

RABBITS' HOME

PICNIC SPOT

PRAIRIE

LESTER'S HOUSE

# Lonesome Lester

by Ida Luttrell   Illustrated by Megan Lloyd

Harper & Row, Publishers

To Bill,
who is my very best friend
I.L.


To Grandma and Grandpa
M.L.

LONESOME LESTER
Text copyright © 1984 by Ida Luttrell
Illustrations copyright © 1984 by Megan Lloyd
Printed in the U.S.A. All rights reserved.

Library of Congress Cataloging in Publication Data
Luttrell, Ida.
  Lonesome Lester.

  Summary: A prairie dog who lives alone discovers the
differences between good company, bad company, and
being peacefully alone.
  [1. Prairie dogs—Fiction.   2. Solitude—Fiction]
I. Lloyd, Megan, ill.   II. Title.
PZ7.L97953Lo 1984      [E]        83-47701
ISBN 0-06-024029-6
ISBN 0-06-024030-X (lib. bdg.)

          1 2 3 4 5 6 7 8 9 10
               First Edition

# Ants

Lester Prairie Dog lived in the last house
on the last street
in the last town
at the edge of the prairie.
On a very still day,
he sat at his table all alone
and ate his supper.

"Sure is quiet today," he said.
"Not one bird singing,
not one bee buzzing.
The wind is not even blowing.
It is just plain lonesome.
Company would be nice."
Then Lester saw something moving.
A string of ants climbed up
onto his table.
"Oh, goody," Lester said. "Company.
Hello, ants, are you hungry?"
The ants marched straight
to the sugar bowl.
"Have some sugar,
but save some for me," Lester said.
The ants climbed into the sugar bowl
and ate all the sugar.

"Hey," said Lester.
"That is just plain greedy."
The ants did not listen.
They marched down the table leg
and across the floor,
leaving sticky tracks behind them.

"Now look, ants, you are making a big mess.
You are greedy and messy," Lester said.
"But company is company."
So Lester cleaned the floor
and went to bed.

The next morning, Lester got out of bed.
He found the ants in his garlic.
They ate all his garlic
and blew their garlic breath everywhere.
"Now, that is just plain rude," said Lester.
"Ants, you are greedy and messy
and bothersome and rude."

5

Lester opened the door.
"So long, ants," he said.
But the ants did not leave.
"Okay, you stay here," said Lester.
"But I won't stay in a house
full of greedy, messy,
bothersome, rude company.
I am going on a picnic."
*Picnic!*

6

The first ant snapped to attention
and passed the word to the very last ant.
The ants watched Lester put sandwiches
and bananas and cookies in a basket.
They watched him pour grape juice into a jar
and put the jar in the basket.
They watched him go out the door.
The ants stopped watching
and started following.

They followed Lester down the trail
through the horsemint
to a clump of sagebrush
in the middle of the prairie.
Lester opened the jar of grape juice
and set it on the ground.
The ants all rushed to get a drink.

Lester picked up his picnic basket,
ran home,
and shut the door tight.

Then he sat down to eat
in his nice quiet, empty house.
"Company is company," he said.
"But that was bad company."

# Aunt Martha

Lester rested in his chair
until the faraway whistle of a train
called him to the window.
"My, that is a lonesome sound,"
Lester said.
"Company would be nice."
Then he heard a tapping
at his front door.

Lester opened the door.
There stood Aunt Martha
wearing a frown,
and smelling of wax and mothballs.
"Hello, Aunt Martha. Come in," Lester said.
"I will," said Aunt Martha.
She stepped inside
and looked around the room.

"Your windows are open, Lester,"
said Aunt Martha.
"I know," Lester said.
"Open windows let in sunshine
and fresh air."
"And dust and mosquitoes," said Aunt Martha.
"You had best close them."
"I like them open," said Lester.
But, company is company, he thought.
So he closed all the windows.

Aunt Martha pointed to the fireplace.
"Do I see peacock feathers
on your hearth?" she asked.
"Yes," Lester said proudly,
"I got them at the fair."
"Quick, take them outside,"
Aunt Martha snapped. "They bring bad luck."
"I think they are pretty," said Lester.
But he took the peacock feathers outside.

Aunt Martha looked under the rug
and behind the sofa.
"It is a good thing
I brought my wax with me," she said.
"This place needs a good waxing."
"But I just cleaned it yesterday,"
said Lester.
"It doesn't shine," said Aunt Martha.
"A waxed house is a shiny house.
And a shiny house is a healthy house,"
she said. "This is not a healthy house."
Aunt Martha took the wax
from her purse.
Lester looked at Aunt Martha
and her wax.
"I like it the way it is," he said,
"but wax it if you like.
I think I will weed my garden."
Aunt Martha waxed the floors,
she waxed the furniture,
and she waxed the porch swing.

She was waxing the porch
when Lester returned from his garden.
"I am tired," Lester said,
and he sat down on the porch swing.
"Don't sit on that swing!"
cried Aunt Martha. "I just waxed it."

Lester got up.
He went to the kitchen
to get a drink.
"Don't walk on that floor,"
cried Aunt Martha. "I just waxed it."

"Aunt Martha," said Lester,
dizzy from wax fumes,
"I think this house
is getting too healthy.
There is a grand opening
of a new store in town.
Wouldn't you like to go?"
"I don't care about new stores,"
said Aunt Martha,
looking for something else to wax.

"They are giving away
free hot dogs,"
said Lester.
"I am not hungry," said Aunt Martha,
waxing the mirror.
"And free soda pop," said Lester.
"I am not thirsty," said Aunt Martha,
waxing behind the mirror.
"And they are having
a special sale on wax," said Lester.
Aunt Martha grabbed her purse.
"I'm going," she said.
Lester opened the door,
and Aunt Martha was gone.
Lester opened all his windows
and put his peacock feathers
back on the hearth.
"Company is company," Lester said.
"But that company was too waxy."

# Baby Rabbit

The next day, Lester stepped outside
to look at the morning
and found it filled with fog.

The fog rolled and swirled
and hid the sun and the prairie.
"It looks mighty lonesome.
All I can see is fog," said Lester.
"Company would be nice."
Suddenly Lester heard a noise.
He followed the noise until
he found Baby Rabbit, all alone,
crying in the fog.

"It looks like somebody is lost,"
Lester said.
Baby Rabbit looked at Lester
and kept on crying.

"When the fog lifts," said Lester,
"we will find your mama."

Lester picked up Baby Rabbit
and carried him home.
Baby Rabbit kept on crying.
"Baby Rabbit, don't cry," said Lester.
"It breaks my heart to hear a baby cry."
Baby Rabbit cried louder.
"I will play games with you," said Lester.
"Then you won't cry."

23

Lester peeked around a chair.
"Peek-a-boo," he said.

"No peek-a-boo!" said Baby Rabbit,
and he cried and sobbed.

Lester clapped his hands.
"Pat-a-cake, pat-a-cake," he said.

"No pat-a-cake!" said Baby Rabbit,
and he screamed and yelled.

"Baby Rabbit, your crying
is breaking my eardrums," Lester said.
"I have done everything but stand on my head."
So Lester stood on his head.
Baby Rabbit looked at Lester and stopped crying.
Baby Rabbit clapped and laughed.

Lester stood on his head
until his neck ached.
Baby Rabbit stopped watching Lester
and began playing with his toes.
"Oh good," Lester said.
"Now you are happy."

Lester put his feet back on the floor.
Baby Rabbit squalled.
"Baby Rabbit," Lester said,
"your crying is breaking my neck."
Just then Lester felt something warm on his back.
"*Sunshine!*" he cried happily.
"The fog is gone."
He picked up Baby Rabbit
and hurried to the door.

And there was Mama Rabbit
coming up the trail!
"Mama!" Baby Rabbit cried.
Mama Rabbit hugged and kissed Baby Rabbit.
"Thank goodness, Lester,
you have found my baby.
I looked and looked for him
until I am plain worn out!"
"Come in and sit down," said Lester,
"I will bring you some grape juice."

"Wonderful!" said Mama Rabbit.
Lester poured grape juice
for Mama Rabbit and Baby Rabbit.

"More," Baby Rabbit said.
"No, no, Baby," said Mama Rabbit,
"We must save some for Lester."
Baby Rabbit looked up at Lester
and said, "Peek-a-boo?"
Lester laughed.

Baby Rabbit played peek-a-boo
and tag with Lester.
"What a shiny, airy, happy home
you have, Lester," said Mama Rabbit.
"Thank you," Lester said, smiling.
"Come and see me again sometime."

"We will," said Mama Rabbit,
"but now we must go."
"Company is company," Lester said
to himself as he waved good-by,
"and *that* is what I call
good company."

# Lester

Lester closed the door
behind Mama Rabbit and Baby Rabbit.
"All alone again," he said.
But he hummed while he put
the juice glasses away
and set his house in order.

He whistled while he hammered
a loose board on his steps
and watered his garden.

He worked a word scramble
while he ate his supper.
He laughed when it spelled out,
"New shoes for old gnus."

And he sang a loud happy song
when he took a bath.

Then he sat on his porch swing
to watch the night come.
A fat, orange moon slid up
over the horizon.

"My, what a nice lonesome sight,"
Lester said. "A full moon all by itself
in a big, dark sky."
A coyote sang a lonely song.
"My, what a nice lonesome sound,"
Lester said. "A coyote, all alone,
singing in the evening."

A breeze stirred and carried
the scent of horsemint from the prairie.
"My, what a nice lonesome smell,"
said Lester. "Horsemint blooming
in an empty field.
But I am not lonesome."
And as he rocked
back and forth on his swing,
Lester thought, "There is good company,
and there is bad company.
But sometimes no company
is just plain peaceful."

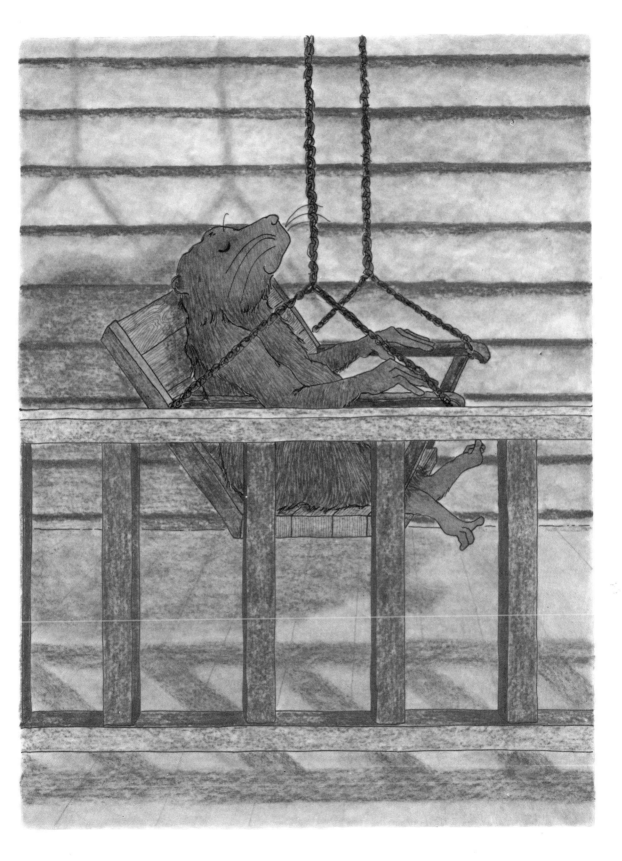

TRAIN STATION

TOWN

STORE

AUNT MARTHA'S HOUSE